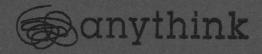

MR. COMPLAIN TAKES THE TRAIN

Wade Bradford
& S. britt

Clarion Books

Houghton Mifflin Harcourt

Boston   New York

Clarion Books
3 Park Avenue
New York, New York 10016

Text copyright © 2021 by Wade Bradford
Illustrations copyright © 2021 by Stephan Britt

Clarion Books is an imprint of Houghton Mifflin Harcourt Publishing Company.

hmhbooks.com

The illustrations in this book were rendered in ink on board and colorized using mixed media.
Coloring–Carlyn Beccia.
The text was set in Chaloops Medium.

Library of Congress Cataloging-in-Publication Data
Names: Bradford, Wade, author. | britt, S., illustrator.
Title: Mr. Complain takes the train by Wade Bradford ; illustrated by Stephan Britt.
Other titles: Mister Complain takes the train
Description: Boston ; New York : Clarion Books/Houghton Mifflin Harcourt,
[2018] | Summary: Mr. Complain always has something to grumble about, even
as he takes a spectacular train ride through mountains, volcanoes, caves,
and oceans, but as his trip comes to an end he realizes he genuinely
enjoyed the journey and is ready to go again.
Identifiers: LCCN 2017010256 | ISBN 9780544829817 (hardcover)
Subjects: | CYAC: Railroad trains–Fiction. | Animals–Fiction.
Classification: LCC PZ7.B7229 Mr 2018 | DDC [E]–dc23
LC record available at https://lccn.loc.gov/2017010256

Manufactured in China
SCP 10 9 8 7 6 5 4 3 2 1
4500811160

To Parker, Cooper, and Carson —**W.B.**

'Tis better to complain, than to arrive —**S.B.**